CLASSICS IN ACTION
ROBIN HOOD

A legend re-told by
Rosalind Sutton

Illustrated by Eric F. Rowe

BRIMAX BOOKS · CAMBRIDGE · ENGLAND

In Sherwood Forest

The forest was silent. Suddenly, horses' hooves pounded down the glade. Robin Hood and his friend, Will Scarlet, rode at a gallop towards a clearing and an enormous oak tree. As the horses slowed down the men raised their arms, grabbed a low branch and swung themselves up; then climbed still higher into thicker foliage. The horses disappeared into the undergrowth; they knew their way home.

There was more galloping and angry voices.

"This way!"

"No! Take the right fork!" Three Norman soldiers drew in.

"We've lost them!" cried one in disgust.

"We should have turned left!" argued another.

"They're here – somewhere . . . Dismount! Find them!" ordered the third.

Robin and Will looked at one another. This was dangerous. These soldiers of the Sheriff of Nottingham must not find their secret valley; must never know that this hollow oak marked the entrance.

Two soldiers walked farther away while the third came to the tree.

"Look at this!" he called. "Come and look!" He stepped in. "It's absolutely holl!"

He didn't finish the word. As he glanced up, an arrow pierced his throat, pinning him to the inside bark.

The other two looked round at his call but, not seeing him went on with their search.

"Fresh hoof-marks here!" shouted one and they both moved closer to the wall of saplings and bushes that hid the gap into the valley. Robin and Will crept along the branches, positioned themselves above the men and waited, timing their attack to a split second.

Then, down they leapt landing astride each soldier's back – gripping with their legs pick-a-back fashion, pulling back a helmet with one hand and driving home a shining blade with the other.

It was done; the daggers had penetrated between helmet and mail. The soldiers lay dead. No information would be carried back to the sheriff. Robin Hood's hide-out was still safe from his chief enemy.

The Sheriff of Nottingham

High above the town, in his great fortress, the sheriff waited for his soldiers – they would bring him Robin Hood – a prisoner at last. Time dragged. Surely the dolts hadn't lost him?

He paced up and down the fine rooms of Nottingham Castle; the castle built by William of Normandy soon after 1066. Since then, the Saxons of England had had a miserable existence. The Norman barons ruled them, taxed them, robbed them of their farms and hanged them for killing a deer or a rabbit.

Even now, in Robin Hood's time at the end of the twelfth century, things were no better. This evil, greedy sheriff had trumped up charges against Robin, taken over his lands and property, put a price on his head and so forced him to become an outlaw.

Many men had suffered in this way. Some had banded together under Robin's leadership and, dressed in their suits of Lincoln green, made their home in Sherwood Forest. They all swore to bring the sheriff down, to trick and pester him; they vowed to help the poor and the ill-treated.

In the forest they had plenty of chances to waylay wealthy travellers. They'd drop down from their hiding places in the trees.

"Your money bags, kind sirs," they would say politely. "Just hand over your gold and we will lead you to safety!"

Robbing monks gave them a special satisfaction for these men had forgotten their vocation; they were interested only in amassing fortunes for their monasteries. They also badgered the sheriff about Robin Hood.

"Catch the villain!" they cried. No wonder Robin enjoyed taking their fat purses.

"How kind!" he would say. "Your generous gift will feed the poor. They will bless you. A pleasant journey to you!" And he would hand them back enough money for a night's lodging.

So the people looked to Robin in all their problems. Besides those who lived with him in the forest, there were many from the villages who would come at his bugle-call. They loved him and they, too, hated the sheriff.

If only they could have seen his worship now – fretting and fuming for his soldiers who would never return.

King Richard off on a crusade

While the sheriff raged in his castle, Robin and Will Scarlet sat under the great oak – their trysting tree. They were filling in the story of their latest adventure and re-living the excitement of it all.

Only the day before, Robin and Will had ridden south to wave King Richard off on a Crusade. How splendid he had looked at the head of his army, a force of both Norman and Saxon soldiers, all going east to fight for the Christians in Jerusalem.

How the people had shouted and waved.

"God bless King Richard! . . ." "Lion-heart! . . . Our Richard Lion-heart! . . ." "Come back to us soon! We need you!"

They gave him a rousing send-off but, yes, they did need him. He would control the barons; he would be a fair man. That had been their hope: now, Prince John would be regent and they dreaded it.

Yes, the barons would do as they pleased, for Prince John was too spineless to stop them.

Robin wasn't worrying about it just now; he was more interested in talking of Richard.

"We were so excited," he said. "They all looked magnificent! And there was the king – quite close!"

"Yes," laughed Will. "Someone else was quite close too – the sheriff! He sent four soldiers after us. And we'd left our horses at the tavern!"

"How we got through that crowd!" went on Robin. "We were down on all fours. Crawling behind the women's skirts and under horses' bellies! That fooled them!"

"Diving into the tavern helped," added Will. "We were out to the stable, mounted and away!"

Robin broke in again. "The chase was on . . . and they were gaining. We slipped into a field just as the farmer let his cows out – that caused havoc! We could hear the soldiers cursing and swearing!"

Robin's men were enjoying the story. Much the Miller's son wished he'd been there and Will Stutely wanted every detail.

"Where were you by this time?" he asked.

"Coming along the Roman road," Robin answered. "Villagers rushed out to look – chickens and

geese scattered everywhere! We
got ahead then and spent the
night in a church south of Newark.
It seemed we had lost them but –"
"There they were," said Will,
"waiting for us on the edge of
the forest: I've never ridden
so fast in my life!"

"Nor I," said Robin. "And if
Will hadn't killed the soldier in
the tree we'd all be searching
for a new home tonight."

"What happened to the fourth?"
asked Much. "You said there
were four soldiers."

"Ah . . . yes . . . he must have
cast a shoe. He dropped out
yesterday. Hallo!" cried Robin,
looking through the trees. "Who is
this?"

A flash of colour moved in the
distance.

"Keep out of sight," he warned
his men. "I'll challenge our
visitor on my own." Robin strode
off to meet the stranger.

Robin meets Little John

On the other side of the stream, an extremely tall man with a thick stick was about to cross by the tree-trunk bridge. Robin stood in his way.

"Let me pass," demanded the stranger.

Robin was ready for a scrap. "I'll fight you first!" he cried.

"You're a fool!" answered the man. "I could knock you senseless with one blow!"

Robin laughed, reaching for an arrow: "Ha! This would split your heart in two – before you hit me!"

The stranger was angry. "A coward too, eh? You threaten with arrows when I have only a stick?"

"Very well, I'll have a stick!" Robin declared as he ran to cut a strong sapling from the bank. "See, we meet on equal terms! How does that suit you?" and he gave the stranger a mighty whack.

"AND that! and THAT!"

Blows fell fast. Robin was quicker – getting in from every direction; but the tall man had more weight and Robin was soon streaming with blood. But he wasn't finished – yet.

Suddenly, a terrific broadside lifted Robin off his feet and sent him sprawling into the deep water. His opponent crossed to the bank.

"Where are you, friend?" he called.

"Swimming against the tide!" came the answer as Robin surfaced and grabbed the hand held out to him. There they stood grinning at one another while Robin's men drew in behind him ready to seize the stranger.

"Let's give him a ducking!" they shouted.

"No!" said Robin. "He fought fairly – with the strength of ten!" He turned to the man. "We could do with you," he added. "How would you like to join us? We have a good life here in the forest. I am Robin Hood."

"Why! You are the very man I came to find! I'd be proud to join you." Once more he offered his hand. "My name is John Little."

The men roared with laughter. "That won't do! You'll have to re-christen him, master!"

"Yes," Robin agreed. "You'll be my right-hand man and I'll call you Little John."

That caused more laughter and back they went to supper and to exchange any news they may have heard lately.

Hubert of The Glen told of an important traveller arriving at Nottingham Castle the next day. "Who is he, then?" asked Robin. He wasn't particularly interested. He felt weary after his bout with Little John.

"A lady, master," Hubert answered.

"Do I know her? Oh, come on, Hubert, out with it!" cried Robin.

"You know her father, master. You befriended him once – Sir Richard of Lea."

"What! Maid Marion coming to the castle? What else have you heard?" Robin demanded.

"They say," went on Hubert, "that Sir Richard rode south today – gathering an army. He plans to join the king. His daughter will be the sheriff's ward until he gets back."

Robin was interested now. The whole thing smacked of treachery. Why would the sheriff help in this way?

Robin thanked Hubert. "You're a good man," he said. "I shall need you in the morning."

Maid Marion's journey

Very early next morning, Robin and Little John, followed by Will Scarlet, Stutely and Hubert, were on their way. They rode to the edge of the forest. This was the way the waggons would come to bring Maid Marion and her women to Nottingham Castle.

Robin sent Stutely out of sight with the horses while he and the others hid in the bushes and trees.

They hadn't been waiting long when several ruffians appeared and started making holes and ruts across the track. They covered these with leaves and grasses. Robin watched closely.

The men then hid – fortunately on the opposite side of the clearing.

Sometime later, the line of waggons approached. Two riders led, using the grass edge. They would be well ahead when the others came to grief. Then came two open carts carrying women and several trunks. A more elaborate, covered waggon followed. Two carts of servants and belongings, and two last riders completed the escort.

Suddenly, complete confusion! Women screamed, horses reared and wheels trundled away. Maid Marion stepped out and the robber gang burst from their hiding places.

Whizz! Whizz! Whizz! Three arrows pierced three men. Two lay dead and one helpless with an arrow in his leg. The others took to their heels.

Robin helped Maid Marion while Will and Hubert took the wounded man prisoner. The outriders calmed horses and servants; Little John had the carts upright and collected scattered boxes.

Meanwhile Robin took Lady Marion aside to talk to her. "I am Robin Hood, my lady, and a friend of Sir Richard, your father."

Marion smiled. "Yes, I have heard my father speak of you. Aren't you Robin of Locksley?"

"I was," he answered, "but I am now dispossessed – an outlaw. Until I earn my pardon from King Richard I am a hunted man and no one is more determined to catch me than the Sheriff of Nottingham."

"I am travelling to his home, now," said Maid Marion. "I shall be staying at the castle until my father returns from the Crusade. Do you wish me to keep our meeting secret?"

"I would be grateful, for your sake," Robin admitted. "And please, I beg you, don't trust this guardian of yours. If ever you need help get word to me. Much the Miller's son delivers flour to the castle; he would bring a message."

"Thank you, I will remember. I think they are ready to move off."

Robin led her to her waggon and bowed his farewell. He was determined to find out the sheriff's game of intrigue and to bring it all to nothing.

The prisoner

The waggons moved off and Robin saw them safely out of the forest. He then gave his attention to the prisoner, a miserable creature who was quite ready to tell all he knew if only his life were spared.

"Who put you up to this?" Robin demanded.

"I don't rightly know – a bailiff in the castle – said we'd be well paid. 'Just get the lady's jewels,' he said. 'No harm to the lady.' He were strict about that. I meant no harm, sir!"

"You wretch!" cried Robin. "She could have broken her neck! Get the arrow out, Will."

The man screamed as Will dealt with it and bound up the wound.

"You'll remember your work today and that's all you'll have as payment – a crippled leg.

Show that to your master!" said Robin sternly. "Now go! I might change my mind and finish you off!"

Stutely rejoined them and they rode towards the valley. But all plans against the sheriff were pushed aside when they saw a young man lying under a tree. He seemed to be in great trouble for he cried out and beat the ground with his fist. A harp stood nearby.

Alan-A-Dale
and his wedding

Robin went to him. "Come, man, what ails you? Can we help?"

The young man looked up – rather scared at the strangers around him. Robin soon won his confidence and sat there hearing his story.

"My name is Alan-a-Dale. I'm a minstrel and I travel to farms and lonely homes. People are glad to welcome me and to hear my songs."

"A good life," said Robin. "What went wrong?"

"Sometime ago," went on Alan, "I met a farmer's daughter, Alice. We fell in love; but her father has arranged her marriage for tomorrow! To an old man – Alan Marsden. Old enough to be her grandfather! I can do nothing to save her. Nothing!"

Robin was interested. He would like to help and it could be an adventure.

"You alone can do nothing," he said, "but together we might do quite a lot. You want to marry your Alice? And she, you?"

Alan was quite sure of that.

"Very well," Robin decided. "Cheer up, young Alan-a-Dale! Alice is not lost – yet! Come with us and have food. A good song will pay for all. Tell us the church and the time. I think we can trick her father and

your rival and have you married in no time at all."

The next day, two men, smart soldiers of the sheriff and a third in Lincoln green – their prisoner – rode towards the Marsden farms. Meanwhile things were happening at Woodstone Church; well before time all the front pews were filled. The bridegroom himself in a splendid cloak with a high collar waited patiently for his bride to appear. A minstrel at the chancel steps plucked gently on his harp.

At last the bishop came and stood ready to conduct the service. Alice entered with her

father and they walked down the aisle. Pale and sad, she stared straight in front of her. The bishop read the vows; these were repeated in turn by the couple. When it was time to plight their troth, the bridegroom took her hand. His hand felt familiar; a young, strong hand. Alice looked up and met the gaze of Alan-a-Dale. The disguise, grey beard and hair, croaking voice – nothing could hide him from her.

As soon as the bride and groom left the altar the people in the front seats followed them to the vestry. Much to the surprise of the bishop and the other dignitaries the happy pair were out and away on horseback.

Alice's father struggled to get through. People were blocking the way.

"What's going on?" he demanded. "I have a banquet waiting. Where are they?"

The south door of the church burst open. In tottered the real bridegroom – Alan Marsden. Voices and tempers flared. The old man tried to explain.

"The sheriff's soldiers directed us to the next village," he protested. "They warned us of Robin Hood! They even had one outlaw as prisoner!"

"Rubbish!" declared the father.

"My daughter has been given in marriage! I gave her! And she's gone! Get after her, you doddering old fool!"

Both farmers looked round for their friends to help: the church was empty. When a party did set off to chase the runaways there was no sign of them.

The uninvited guest

Mistress Alice and her husband, Alan-a-Dale, were safe in the outlaw's valley. And their banquet?

Well, it wasn't the one Alice had expected, but one she would never forget. Prepared by Robin's men, it was all feasting, laughing and dancing.

How Robin was teased about his performance as a minstrel! How they laughed at Will Stutely, imitating Alan Marsden who had turned tail immediately at the mention of Robin Hood!

Alice thanked Robin for his clever plot and examined Alan's disguise.

"But I would have known," she declared, "had I looked. I thought Marsden stood there – I certainly didn't want to look at him!"

"I depended on that," said Robin. "If you had recognized him too soon, the whole thing might have fallen apart."

"What gave you the idea?" Alice asked.

"They have the same name," he replied. "Only Christian names are used in the marriage service. We were lucky."

Robin claimed a dance with the bride; Alan's songs filled the valley and the celebrations went on through the night. They had made friends for life, these two, and would often return to find an enthusiastic audience ready to enjoy their company.

Towards dawn, when the party was nearly over, Robin wandered out to the great oak. He climbed up and gazed round the forest.

A short distance away, on a slight rise, he saw a Norman soldier and his mount. Motionless they were – a statue silhouetted against the pale sky. The sheriff's fourth rider had found the camp!

Robin and Dirk

Robin too, kept still. He had no weapons; he watched and waited.

It seemed the soldier was listening to Alan-a-Dale's last song. When the music faded, he turned his horse and rode slowly away.

Robin was down, into the camp and pulling Much to one side.

"Quick," he whispered, "help me into a soldier's uniform . . . we have a spy outside. Will! Saddle a Norman's horse – the mare with the blaze – I like her. Quick, man!" He was soon ready and mounted.

"You look very like one of them," said Stutely.

"Good. Keep a lookout," said Robin.

"Take your horn, master," advised Much," – just in case." Robin nodded, took it from him and was gone.

He followed the path the man had taken and then, with a few short cuts, soon had him in sight. Hearing Robin's horse, the soldier turned and hailed him as a friend.

"Thank God, Gamel!" he cried. "Thought you were finished! Where are the others?"

"Resting," Robin answered.

"We must work out an explanation; the sheriff won't excuse this delay – probably has men on our trail already. Any luck with the outlaws?" the soldier added.

"I know where their camp is," said Robin.

"So do I," the man admitted, "but not the actual entrance."

"Shall we tackle them?" asked Robin.

"We'd stand no chance," the man answered. "Besides, I have quite a fellow feeling for this Robin Hood."

"You have?" exclaimed Robin.

"Yes, I have. I'm half Saxon, Gamel, and I've no stomach for some of the sheriff's orders. He's a vicious devil. He'll have us in the dungeons even if we do inform against the outlaws. How if we ride in and offer to join them?"

"What makes you think they'd trust us?" Robin asked.

"Robin Hood isn't stupid – he'd test us. When we've shown our mettle we'd be accepted; comrades with a cause – that's what counts. What did I tell you? See?" Six of the sheriff's men rode towards them.

"We are too late!" moaned the soldier.

"Never!" Robin declared. "Let me handle this. You prove you are against the sheriff and I'll be an outlaw with you!"

"Watch out," warned his companion, "Leo is in charge – he's a brute." They moved to meet the six.

"Well met!" cried Robin. "We need reinforcements."

"You've taken your time!" accused Leo.

"Ah, but we're alive and we've tailed our quarry," Robin replied.

"The others dead then?" he was asked.

"Very dead," said Robin. "Now you can reap the glory. I can take you right to the outlaws' hide-out."

"Is that true, Dirk?" Leo looked hard at the rather uneasy man.

"Of course!" Dirk answered. "Take your orders from him."

"To the stream then!" yelled Robin. "Straight ahead!" Leo's men turned and galloped off. Dirk and Robin followed.

Their way led right past the great oak. Robin knew that Much would be watching so, keeping well behind the others, he pulled out his horn, put it to his lips and then threw it under the tree.

The signal was obvious. Much was passing it on and the men were ready. A few stayed to guard the camp; the rest rode in silence, taking a shorter route to the stream. There, in the trees, they waited watching the spot along the bank where the soldiers would emerge.

Robin left Dirk at the rear while he moved up to lead the six.

"Follow me!" he ordered quietly. He was into the water and moving towards his own men.

Suddenly a horse neighed! Little John's mount had seen its stable companion – the mare with the blaze!

It was time for action. Out burst Robin's men; the fight was on!

With his sword, Robin swung round on Leo, slashing him down on to the bank. A second fell with an arrow through his cheek. John roared his battle cry, leaping into the water, slamming and flaying with his stick. Stutely used his dagger – swift and sure. Will Scarlet on the bank watched for a chance to shoot. He'd get that one on the end. But to his amazement the man was fighting the Normans!

Leo staggered up and was after Robin.

"Look out, Gamel!" shouted Dirk as he flung himself on the leader. Leo fought back like a tiger. Dirk was bleeding but he hung on and with all his strength forced Leo down and down under the red, stained water.

Robin was busy with the last as John watched the two he'd stunned sink below him.

It was over. Clambering up the bank, Robin held out his hand to the soldier who had saved him. "Meet my friend; Dirk," he said to his men. Then turning, he added; "I am sorry about Gamel – he was killed at our camp. I am Robin Hood. Do you still want to join us?"

Dirk was too amazed to answer; the admiration in his face answered for him.

Guy of Gisbourne

Robin decided that Little John must learn to shoot. He'd shown his power with the stick, but one day that might not be enough.

The next morning, Robin and Dirk were in a quiet glade giving John his first lesson, when a terrible scream brought them to a standstill.

"Someone in a trap?" Dirk suggested.

"Let's find out," cried Robin and led the way.

More cries and moans were heard; then an angry voice above a pleading one. The three hid in a thicket and peeped out to see a Norman baron with a whip standing over a poor wretch.

"Guy of Gisbourne," whispered Dirk. "He'd torture his own mother!"

"So," the baron was shouting, "you rob me of my rents – you steal and poach! This will teach you!"

He went on thrashing the man, who could cry and plead no longer. Blood oozed from his face and hands, seeping through his thin shirt.

Robin seethed. Injustice! Cruelty! The man couldn't fight back.

"Get yourselves a switch," said Robin, quietly, "and follow me." He sent an arrow to fall just at Gisbourne's feet. The startled baron looked round. In a flash Robin was there, snatching the whip and giving him a taste of the same treatment.

"Now!" he cried, "let's hear _you_ plead for mercy!"

He brought the lash down to skim across Gisbourne's face. Then, Dirk and John were there, and all three teased and tormented him. Jumping and dodging, Gisbourne raged with frustration.

"Just what I'd expect from outlaw scum!" he sneered. "Three to one!"

"Weren't you three to one against the peasant?" demanded Robin. "Your strength, your weapon and of course, your – nobility?"

Gisbourne was silent: there was no answer to that accusation. Robin snapped the whip handle across his knee and threw the pieces away.

"Go home, Norman tyrant!" he cried. "Nurse your one cut! Don't tell anyone how you came by it! They might laugh at you!"

Dirk and John tickled his heels as he struggled to mount. Never had Gisbourne been so humiliated; never had he felt more determined to get his revenge.

Robin turned to the man on the ground. His wife had appeared and was crying over him. "Where do you live?" asked Robin as he helped her up. "Please lead the way."

Little John carried the man and they wended their way to her poor cottage.

"He'll be all right," said Robin.

"Bathe his cuts with boiled, salt water. Here, pay your rent if Gisbourne sends his steward," and he gave her two pieces of gold.

"Your husband needs rest and good food. One of my men will bring you fresh meat each day."

"God bless you, sir! Please, will you tell me who you are?"

Robin turned as they left the tumble-down dwelling. "They call me Robin Hood," he said.

The three men walked away. Little John couldn't contain his feelings any longer.

"You should have killed him!" he cried. "That Gisbourne! He's not fit to live!"

"You missed a good chance," added Dirk.

"The peasant might have been blamed — and hanged. I couldn't risk that," Robin said quietly.

"Do you know," laughed Dirk, "I told you, Gamel, only yesterday, Robin Hood isn't stupid!"

Robin grinned. Joking and laughing, they went back to teach John archery.

The fighting Friar

Little John practised at the butts everyday and soon acquired sufficient skill to shoot with the others. All Robin's men enjoyed their bouts against one another, and the friendly insults that contributed to the fun. Robin was proud of his band.

"Why," he remarked, "if I travel the country I'll not find better bowmen."

Will Scarlet laughed. "You are wrong, master," he explained. "There's a friar, in Fountains Dale, who can outshoot the best of us – AND put us to shame with the sword."

"Then I must meet him," declared Robin. "Where is he?"

"Not so fast," Will advised. "You'll need your mail against Friar Tuck."

Robin was impatient, but only when he was well covered and well armed would Scarlet show him the way. At the ford the stream ran swift and deep.

"Leave me now, Will. I'll meet this man alone."

Robin could see the friar sitting outside his cave eating an enormous pie. And what a man! Little John was indeed little compared to him.

"Friar!" Robin called to him. "Will you carry me over the stream?"

The friar looked up, put down his pie and came to the water's edge. He carefully tucked up his habit and without a word waded towards Robin. There he offered his back and carried the outlaw over. As soon as they were both on the bank the friar spoke.

"Now, good sir, do me the courtesy of carrying me across as I have done for you."

Robin could hardly refuse. It took all his strength but he didn't give in. Swaying and bending under the great weight, he struggled to reach the other side.

They were both extremely polite, but the glint in their eyes told a different story.

"Now, good friar," said Robin, "be so good as to carry me back again."

Smiling to himself, Friar Tuck once more offered his back. Robin was regaining his breath and planning an attack on this giant when, suddenly, he was tossed over the friar's head and into the stream. "If you want my side – swim for it!" he was told.

Out of the water they turned on each other. Swords were drawn – the battle began. Blow followed blow – slash and crash! The struggle seemed to go on for hours with never a let-up. Sliding and teetering at the edge of the stream they pulled back . . . recovered and were at it again!

Finally, they both slumped to the ground – completely exhausted.

"Allow me, good friar, to blow my horn," gasped Robin at last. In seconds, there stood Little John, Will, Dirk and several others, all ready to defend him.

"Allow me, good fellow, to whistle," said the friar as he raised fingers to his mouth. Suddenly, a pack of huge dogs bounded from the cave and hurtled towards the men. In self-defence, they replied with arrows. But, incredibly, the dogs leapt and snatched at the arrows as if bringing back sticks for their master.

"Call off your dogs!" yelled Will. The friar did nothing.

"We'll shoot to kill!" threatened John.

The friar spoke quietly, patting his thigh. "Here, Christian! . . . Turk!" Two dogs went to sit by him. "Now, Norman! . . . Saxon!" They, too, lay at his feet.

"Never hurt them," warned Friar Tuck, "they are true friends. And who are these?"

"My men," Robin answered. "I am Robin Hood and we live in the forest. I have never met a man of your strength and skill. Will you join our band, wear Lincoln green and live with us? We lead a happy life – we're true comrades."

The friar looked round at them. "Huntsmen, I see. Good. Food is important to me. You are a brave man, Robin . . . Yes, I'll be pleased to join you. I was, for many years, at Fountains Abbey; but the people there became corrupt and unjust, so I became a hermit. Now, you offer me friendship and a free life. I am fortunate. Thank you."

Friar Tuck gathered his few belongings together and with his dogs went with Robin. In the glade, he built himself a shelter and became one of the Merry Men. Usually he wore his simple one-piece gown and still thought of himself as a friar. People in the villages liked and respected him; to them he was always "Father".

Robin confides in Friar Tuck

The more Robin came to know Friar Tuck the more he trusted and admired him. One evening he told him about Maid Marion and his suspicions of the Sheriff of Nottingham.

"I know the Lady Marion," said the friar. "She stayed at the convent near Fountains Dale as a young girl. I wonder Sir Richard didn't leave her there during his absence."

"I think the sheriff has Sir Richard in his power," answered Robin. "Probably lent him money for his crusade."

"Yes," Tuck agreed. "And Sir Richard will pay dearly for the loan." The friar offered to find out how things were at the castle.

The next day he set out to visit Maid Marion. Much and Will Stutely rode with him. As they approached the town, Stutely took charge of the horses, while Tuck and Much walked on to the castle.

At Nottingham Castle

The servants welcomed Much; he was a pleasant fellow. While he took food and drink he noticed Grace, a kitchen maid, setting a small portion on an extra platter.

"Who's that for then?" he asked. "You're trying to starve him, surely?"

"Poor man," said Grace, "he's not well. Here, you take it, Much. I can't bear those dungeons. You won't be stopped; the guard has slipped out for half an hour."

"How about the others?" asked Much.

"There are no others," Grace answered. "The sheriff has sent them off to Newark with the rest of the prisoners – a hanging, as a treat for Prince John while he is there. So there's only this one prisoner; a child could mind him."

"Who is he?" Much asked.

"I don't know; but he's a gentleman, and so kind. Have a word with him, Much. Cheer him up a bit." Grace gave him the wooden dish and the keys, and led the way to the top of the steps.

"Mind," she warned, "it's very slippery – and it gets worse as you go down lower . . . Are you scared of rats?"

"Rats too?" gasped Much. "How can the sheriff put anyone in such a place!"

"You don't know the sheriff" said Grace as she returned to the kitchen.

Much felt his way down the slimy steps. The rush lamps at each turn of the stone stairs gave just enough light to show the vile sweating walls, and the eyes of dark creatures darting away from his feet.

Down . . . down . . . and down. He knew the castle was riddled with caves and dungeons; he'd never imagined anything as ghastly as this. He pictured himself a prisoner; away from the forest, the light and warmth of the sun – and from his friends. Could a man survive and not go mad?

At the bottom, Much struggled to open a heavy door. Stench and darkness hit him. It was terrifying. He backed out, took a lamp from the wall and entered slowly.

There, on a straw pallet, lay a figure – alive or dead he didn't know; it kept so still.

Much makes a discovery

"I've brought food, sir. May I help you to a little?" Much spoke gently: The prisoner turned at his voice.

"You sound different. Who are you, my good fellow?"

Much was filled with pity. "I am Much, the Miller's son, sir. I've brought your meal; the maid hates the rats."

The poor man actually smiled. "I don't mind them now. They are companions – in the dark . . . Haven't I seen you somewhere before?"

"Possibly," answered Much. "If you would tell me your name and why you are a prisoner, I might be able to help you."

The man's face lit up. "If only you could!" he exclaimed.

"If you could get word to the Sheriff of Nottingham he'd come at once and get me out of here. Some villains said I was against Prince John. I gathered men to help King Richard! The sheriff knows about my Crusade. Will you get word to him? And to my daughter? Can you, please?"

Much was staggered. This poor creature was Sir Richard of Lea! He didn't know it was the sheriff who held him prisoner in the very castle where Maid Marion was staying! What could he tell him?

"I'm sorry," went on, Sir Richard, "it is too much to ask. The journey would be long and full of danger."

He shrank back – more hopeless than ever.

"No, sir, that isn't so at all. Help is nearer than you think. You *have* seen me before – I am one of Robin Hood's men."

"What!" cried the prisoner, "What are you doing in Kent?"

"You are not in Kent, sir – you think this is Dover Castle?"

"Of course!" Sir Richard answered.

"Sir," Much started slowly, "I have to tell you of great – no, of evil treachery . . . Are you strong enough to bear it?"

Sir Richard looked at him. "I can bear the truth," he said.

"Please take some food. It will help you, sir. And remember, Robin Hood and all his men are at your service."

So, while Sir Richard ate, Much told the story as far as he knew it. The minutes slipped by; he had to get back to the kitchen. He left Sir Richard with plenty to think about, and with hope and determination to live to face the sheriff.

Friar Tuck and Maid Marion

In a room high up in the castle, Maid Marion was talking to her old friend Friar Tuck. He asked after her father and learned that she had received no news from him.

When the lady-in-waiting went to bring refreshment for the friar he spoke of Robin Hood. "He begs you to tell me if there is any way in which he can help you."

"Bring me word of my father," she asked. "That is my chief concern. One other thing; do you know Guy of Gisbourne? He is a constant visitor here and greatly admired by my guardian. In fact I'm being persuaded to accept Sir Guy in marriage. He is amusing and charming, and yet. . ."

"And yet?" prompted Friar Tuck.

"I feel he is too good to be true. Do you know what I mean?"

The friar smiled. "I do indeed; your instinct is quite right. Don't enter into any contract – either with Sir Guy or the sheriff."

While the friar took wine, Marion told him of the coming tournament. "It's to be quite splendid. I do hope you and your friends will be able to come."

"I hope so, too," he answered. "I will come again soon and bring you news of Sir Richard."

Leaving the castle, he found Stutely waiting, and Much bursting to tell of his discovery.

"Wait," ordered Tuck. "Even the trees have ears." So, nothing was discussed until that evening when Robin heard it all.

"What a plot!" he cried. "He wants her father to die in that appalling place! Then to give – no, to sell his ward to that villain, Gisbourne. God in Heaven! What can we do?"

They had plenty of ideas but no sure way of getting Sir Richard out of the castle.

"Sleep on it, master," advised Little John. "Sleep sorts most things out."

Robin gets an idea

Sleep. Robin had little that night and by dawn he was wandering through the forest. He saw nothing of the beauty around him; only the misery of his friend and the crafty Gisbourne trying to impress his Maid Marion.
His? His Maid Marion?
He came to a standstill. Yes, he had, for a long time, treasured the thought of Marion. He knew now, quite surely, that one day she would be his bride. Nothing was impossible – he would find a way!

Then he saw it – a hovel built into a cave. And painted on the rotting door, a cross. It was the sign of the plague!

For some minutes he gazed. Here was an idea. Nothing was formed or clear but he felt in his bones that he had found the answer. He sat with his back against a tree, resting his head and arms on his knees. The hours passed unnoticed.

A friend in need

Towards midday, a woman came gathering sticks. She stared at Robin sitting there. He was the man who'd helped her!

"Why, sir!" she cried. "Are you all right?"

It was some seconds before he recognized her. "Oh, it's you. How is your husband?"

The woman smiled. "Better, sir, thank you. Begging your pardon, sir, he wants to join your followers. Would that be possible, sir?" Robin hardly heard her. "When was the plague in there?" he asked, looking towards the hovel.

"Oh, that! Why, years ago, sir. I was but a child. A soldier it were, back from some war. Taken prisoner by Frederick of Barbarossa. I always remember that name. Plague broke out in the camp and the soldier managed to escape. He didn't escape the scourge, though; brought it back he did, and died in there, poor soul."

"Did the plague spread?" Robin asked.

"No," she answered. "Only to his wife. He'd deserted, you see, so they hid away in there. My father burnt their bodies to protect us children. Never reported it – just put the cross. 'Burning's the only way,' he said and 'Kill all the rats,' he said. He must have been right, too."

Robin nodded. "Yes, he probably was."

Then he was up and ready to go. "Thank you, you've been a friend, when I needed one. Tell your husband – what is his name?"

"John Greenwood, master."

"Well, Mistress Greenwood, tell John that if he hears three blows on my horn, I shall need him. If he comes to my aid, then he shall be one of my men. I'll be glad to welcome him."

The woman's face was all smiles. "Oh, John will be that glad. Good day, sir, Robin Hood, sir!" She was off, dropping sticks as she ran.

The beggar

Robin whistled as he strode along. An idea was taking shape in his mind.

Suddenly, from the bushes, a man stepped out in front of him. "Alms for a poor beggar," he pleaded. "Spare a coin, kind sir."

Robin looked him up and down. His clothes were disgusting – a splendid disguise.

"I have no money," he answered, "but I'll change cloaks with you. What do you say?"

The man's cloak was off in a flash. "The hat too, sir?" ventured the beggar.

Robin was laughing to himself. "By all means! And the shoes. Well – made to measure!" Robin watched him swagger off.

"Probably thinks I'm quite mad," he thought. But there was reason in Robin's madness.

He aged his face with lines and stains of berries and turned towards the village in The Glen. The whole place buzzed with anger and distress. One woman, sitting at her cottage door, wept and moaned.

"Please," said Robin, bending down to her, "what's the matter?. What's going on?"

"My three sons!" she cried.

"See! Bound hand and foot. They're going to hang them – this afternoon!" And she burst out crying again. Robin waited a few seconds.

"What are they accused of?"

"My eldest shot a deer. Not the others. But the sheriff has condemned all three as an example, to others. My poor boys! What can I do?"

Robin seethed with the injustice of it all. "Take courage, mother," he said. "Things could change, you know, at the very last minute."

With that he left her, mingled with the crowd and moved towards the prisoners.

While the guard was busy pushing and cursing the sightseers, Robin slipped behind him.

"Don't be afraid," he encouraged the brothers. "Help will come. The friar will hear your confessions – do as he says."

Robin returned to the forest, summoned his men and gave them their instructions.

The Sheriff is tricked

About half an hour before the hanging was to take place the sheriff and his attendants arrived. From his seat on the platform he looked round for any sign of Lincoln green but there was no sign of any trouble. Robin's men were looking quite ordinary and passed as working men drawn together by the excitement of a hanging.

Robin, bent over like an old man, and still in his disguise, approached the platform.

"Good sir," he appealed to the sheriff, "you are a just man – do not send these villains to eternity before they confess their sins. You will be blessed, sir, if you allow them to make their peace with God."

The sheriff glared at the beggar and was about to send him off. Then, wishing to appear merciful, he said. "You are right, my good fellow. Is there a priest here?"

Robin shielded his eyes.
"My sight is poor, your honour. Can you see one?" If not I'll go and find one . . ."

"Wait," said the sheriff. "There's Friar Tuck on the edge of the crowd."

To everyone's amazement he asked the friar to come forward. The sheriff was a just man after all!

When Friar Tuck saw the men's hands bound behind them he asked that the cords be cut. Then, sending the guard to one side, he went to the eldest brother. While hearing his confession he placed his hands on those of the prisoner and slipped him a small, sharp knife.

"When the arrows fall, cut free. Make for the forest and follow the beggar."

He blessed each one, then turned to bow to the sheriff. As he did so arrows rained down! There was complete and utter confusion. The sheriff bolted, and the villagers fell over each other as they fought to get away. Meanwhile the prisoners had disappeared.

As they entered the forest, the beggar waved them on and with remarkable speed led them to the great oak. There, he told them who he was and offered them a place in his band of outlaws. He had tricked the sheriff. Could he trick him again? Yes! When his plan was ready, he'd certainly make a fool of the Sheriff of Nottingham.

That night, Robin told Friar Tuck what he planned.

"A clever idea," Tuck agreed. "And it will work – if we get every detail right. Let it rest in our minds. New points will occur to us and we need to discuss them."

Robin agreed to wait a day or two.

A tax for the King's ransom

Next morning, Will Stutely took the widow news of her three sons. She blessed the name of Robin Hood and vowed that if she could ever do him a kindness, he had only to ask.

While Will was talking, several men from the castle rode into the village. Stopping in the centre, a herald read out a proclamation as follows: "Hear ye! Hear ye! Prince John has authorized the honourable Sheriff of Nottingham to levy a new tax of one penny on every man, woman and child.

Bring your tax money here tomorrow morning at the hour of ten. The bailiff will receive all monies. These will help to pay the ransom demanded by Leopold of Austria for the release of our illustrious king, Richard the Lion-Heart!
God save the king!"

The people turned to one another. "We are starving now!" they cried. "What will happen to us if we can't pay?"

They were a poor frightened lot and Will pitied them as he returned to tell Robin the news.

The outlaws collect for the King

Robin and Friar Tuck discussed the new hardship put upon the villagers.

"It so happens," said the friar, "that several monks will journey this way this very afternoon. They will have gold; it is payment day for dues from Newark churches to Fountains Abbey. The men know me so I cannot help. Let Little John wear my habit. He'll fill it out – here and there! He could invite them to a meal, and I'm sure you can plan from there, eh, Robin?"

They both laughed; it was an opportunity not to be missed.

Little John looked the part as he set out to meet the monks from Newark. There were three of them, all tired and hungry and very pleased to accept this friar's invitation.

The supper was excellent; a feast of venison, game and fish. Friar Tuck kept out of sight in the hollow tree. He had his food with him and almost choked over it too think of the surprise these three would soon be getting. He could hear most of their conversation.

"I suppose," Robin was saying, "your Abbey will make a donation to the Ransom Fund?"

"We have many commitments," the eldest monk explained. "But we shall do our best . . . Oh, yes,

we shall do our best."

"Did you know," Robin went on, "that every man has to pay a penny for each one in his family? That could be more than his wage! Did you know that?" The monks were silent.

"Another thing," demanded Robin, "did you know the poor are so underfed that if they sat here with us now, they could take but a few mouthfuls? I'm sure you didn't. Now, you are good men, holy men; I can count on your help for these people. Give, good priests. Pour out the gold you carry. God will bless you."

The holy men were in a flutter. "Gold!" cried one. "We carry no gold!"

"No! No gold!" repeated the others.

"If that is so," said Robin, "of course, you cannot give. But if you are lying – but there, men of God do not lie, surely? Please give a few pence and we will lead you safely on your way."

The monks made ready to mount. "We have nothing; nothing at all!" they declared.

At a glance from Robin his men surrounded them. The monks were up-ended, shaken and placed face down on the ground. Habits were lifted, garments, loosened; pats and proddings followed over their bodies. For the youngest, this was agony; he was extremely ticklish.

Giggling and writhing, he begged for mercy.

"Stop! . . . STOP! . . . PLEASE!" he yelled. "I c . . can't bear any more!"

The outlaws roared with laughter. Robin thought Tuck would burst the tree.

"Oh! . . . Oh! . . . Please!" wailed the poor wriggler . . . "In our s-s-stockings!"

The haul of gold piled up; the dejected monks tidied themselves. The youngest was so exhausted he had to be helped.

"Come," said Robin, offering him wine, "this is probably the best deed you and your brothers have ever done. AND you've given us some good fun."

The monks rode away – slowly They didn't see it quite like that.

For the villagers, it was a miracle – one that Fountains Abbey could well afford.

Robin's plan - first day

Once more, Robin and Friar Tuck went over the plan to rescue Sir Richard. Much made another visit to the castle kitchen and waited for Grace to ask him to go down to the dungeon.

How glad Sir Richard was to see him and how thankful to hear Robin's message.

"Keep a brave heart, sir," said Much, "but to your guard pretend to be ill. Start tonight, and be worse tomorrow. Then, the following morning rave and send him away. Cry out, 'Plague! Unclean! Keep away! It's the plague!' Make the guard very frightened. Can you do that?"

"Yes, anything to get out of here," he answered.

"Later that day," went on Much, "two men will come. You must pretend to be dead – allow them to carry you away. Don't be afraid, it has all been planned by my master. Robin sends his greetings. Your daughter is well and so will you be – quite soon."

Sir Richard laughed. Such news – such wonderful news!

"One thing more," added Much, "what time does your guard make his first round?"

"He usually says, 'Just gone six' or, 'Nearly seven.' It hardly varies," said Sir Richard.

"Thank you. Time is important," said Much.

"I pray you will succeed. God be with you!"

"And you, Sir Richard," and Much came away.

Meanwhile, in the forest, Will Scarlet killed a medium sized deer. He skinned it, put it in a sack which he sewed up, and then hung it from a tree. In the full sun , the meat soon began to smell; it was very objectionable but it was all part of Robin's plan.

That evening, Robin, disguised as the old beggar, went to see the widow in the village.

"I have come to ask a kindness of you, mother," he said.

"Anything, master," she promised. "First," he suggested, "how would you like to see your sons, eh?"

"That would be wonderful!" she cried.

Robin explained that he wanted to borrow her cottage for two or three nights – that she could stay with her sons until she was brought home again.

"When do we leave?" she asked.

"Put a few things together. Now, have you an old cloak? Good. Be ready tomorrow evening. Tell your neighbours you have a sick relative here. Invite no one inside. My men will come for you when it's dark. Bless you, mother, you have no idea what good will come of this."

More preparations

Things were going well – every piece fitting and leading to the final day.

Next morning, Robin became a butcher, in clothes once worn by one of his men. It was market day and Robin waited for the real butcher to come along. Eventually he heard him, far off, singing at the top of his voice.

"Good morning!" he called as the cart drew near. "You sound happy! Is your meat as good as your voice?"

The butcher laughed. "Better, I hope. I need to sell to earn my living – nobody will buy my voice!"

"Well," went on Robin, "I must say it's worth hearing – cheered me up no end. You see, I have no meat from the farmer to supply my customers . . . Would you like to sell me your whole load? I'll give you a fair price."

The man hesitated.

"I tell you what," added Robin, "I shall need your horse and cart. I'll give ten pieces of gold for the lot. Is that fair?"

The man was amazed. For that money he could buy a younger horse, a better cart and twice the amount of meat!

Robin was turning away. "I'm sorry," he said, "I can offer no more."

"That's fine, sir!" called the man. "A good price. I'll make a bargain with you. You have the gold now?"

Robin counted the coins into his hand. The butcher climbed down and Robin drove into the village. Many surprised families had a free joint that day. Finally, Robin returned to the forest.

His men removed the rods and meat hooks and painted out the name of the butcher. It was exactly what Robin needed; a very ordinary, old cart.

That night, as soon as it was dark, Hubert of The Glen, Will Stutely and Will Scarlet rode to the widow's cottage. She knew Hubert as an old neighbour and went quite happily. She locked her door and gave him the key. Safely mounted with him she reached the outlaws' valley. What a welcome they gave her! The fire glowed; delicious smells excited her appetite, and there, to lift her down were Ben, Tom and young Alfred, her dear sons.

After supper they all sang to her, drank to her and praised her courage. At last, under a roof of covered branches and tucked warm between deer-skins, she slept.

Robin and Friar Tuck had their final talk. Hubert had given the friar the widow's key. Her skirt and hooded-cloak were ready for Robin in the morning. The body of the deer lay in the cart, hidden under logs of wood. A clean sack was there to be hidden round Tuck's middle. Little John had a monk's habit to wear; he'd been given his instructions. He and John Greenwood had been working nearly all day in the plague-hovel. Everything was ready for the dawn of the third day.

The guard gets a fright

It was barely light next morning when Friar Tuck, Robin and Little John set out. First, the friar rode off for Nottingham Castle. Then Robin, disguised as an old woman, and John, as a priest, bumped along in the cart to the village. They drove to the back of the widow's cottage and into a thicket. After tethering the horse they hid in the woman's barn to wait.

It was not yet six o'clock when Friar Tuck entered the castle gate near the stables. He had a chat with the farrier who was already busy at his forge. Monks or travelling priests often came to the castle; it was nothing unusual. He left his horse and went on to the kitchen.

47

Grace remembered the smiling friar.

"Good morning, Father," she greeted him. "Come and have some breakfast. Have you come far today?"

"Far enough," he answered. "I'm not built for horse-riding." He was glad to sit at the big table where a guard was gulping down the last of his meal. They exchanged "Good mornings," as the man stood up to go.

"Ah, that's better!" he said, slapping his stomach. "If I don't get some food inside me first, I certainly don't fancy it when I've been down below."

Friar Tuck looked sympathetic. "That bad?" he asked.

"Terrible. The stench!" the guard answered. "Have you come to give the last sacrament, Father?. No? Well, I reckon he could do with it. Not long for this world. Very ill yesterday. Might be dead now – best thing, poor wretch. This platter for him, Grace?" he called to the girl across the great room. "Too much! He'll never eat it. Morning, Father," and he stumped off.

Friar Tuck sat eating while Grace went to re-fill the jug with mead. It was very quiet.

Was Robin right? Would the man be all that frightened? On the next few moments depended the whole fate of their plan. He seemed to have waited hours. It was not working out – that much was obvious. Their efforts had been in vain.

Suddenly, there was a scuffle of feet and the guard burst into the kitchen. "Get out, Father! It's the plague! That man has the plague!" Tuck was up at once, helping the man into the yard.

"Keep calm, my good fellow," he said quietly. "Keep your voice down. Don't let Grace hear you. You can't be sure he has the plague."

"That's what he said! 'Go!' he said. 'I'm unclean! It's the plague! Don't come near! Keep away! Plague!' He said it over and over. I dropped the food and ran. Didn't even lock the door."

The man was so terrified he could hardly stand. The friar helped him to a mounting-block to sit down.

"Don't worry about the door. The poor man's not likely to escape, is he? Now, did you touch the prisoner?"

The guard shook his head.

"Good," went on the friar. "Keep away from other people for a few days. Tell nobody! Not one single soul – you understand? I'll make it right with the sheriff about your desertion – if you promise to do as I say."

The man was in a daze and trembling.

"You do understand?" repeated the friar.

The guard nodded. "Listen carefully," Friar Tuck spoke persuasively. "I have an aunt living in The Glen. I'm using her cottage while she's away from home. You can go there. Are you listening? It is the last one from this end. If you have no swellings or sores in three day's time, you'll be all right. I think I have the key. Ah, yes, take it . . . Now, pull yourself together. You may take my horse.''

The guard managed to walk to the stables where the friar helped him to mount. ''God bless you, my son. Remember your promise.''

''I will, Father, and thank you. Last cottage in The Glen, you say?''

''Yes, there's meal there and mead – you won't starve!'' Friar Tuck gave the horse a friendly slap as the guard rode off.

So far, so good. The friar returned to the kitchen and to his breakfast.

''Thought you'd vanished into thin air, Father!'' laughed Grace.

''What, all this, child?'' he queried, feeling his tremendous girth. ''I may wish I could if the sheriff is in a bad mood. I've just sent his guard on an errand. His honour won't take kindly to that, eh?''

Grace looked quite horrified. ''No, Father. The sheriff does the sending and woe betide . . . Perhaps he need not know?'' she said, hopefully.

''You're a kind lass,'' complimented Tuck. ''I'll sit here and have some mead to bolster my courage.''

She smiled and filled his goblet.

The Friar tackles the Sheriff

To avoid further conversation and to pass a little time, Friar Tuck allowed his several chins to rest comfortably on his chest. Grace got on with her work; maids came and went through the kitchens, and the friar had his cat-nap in peace.

After nearly an hour he went upstairs to find the sheriff. "Ah, my good fellow," he said to a manservant coming towards him, "the sheriff is expecting me. Where do I go, please?"

"Follow me, Father. If you'll pardon the warning, Father, the sheriff is – well – not very happy this morning."

Friar Tuck gave him a friendly grin. "I'll tread carefully, then," he promised.

The sheriff sat at breakfast. He waved the friar into a chair and kept him waiting. Then, pushing his meal away, he looked up. Friar Tuck spoke in a low and serious voice.

"I hope I find you well, my lord sheriff?"

"I have little appetite. I'm pestered with orders from Westminster. 'Do this! Do that! Levy a new tax! Send prisoners! Send fines!' I'm bogged down with it all!"

Friar Tuck nodded in sympathy. "It's too much, sir. And here am I bringing more problems. I'm sorry, but it is of the utmost urgency."

The sheriff scowled and threw up his hands.

"Let's have it then, good friar. Only a death sentence could add to my worries now!" and he laughed at his own gloomy thoughts.

Friar Tuck paused.

"Well?" urged the sheriff.

"You are in good health, my lord? And your servants?"

The sheriff was disturbed. "What is it, man? Not disease? Not plague? Where? Not in the castle?"

The friar had him on the hook nicely.

"I'm afraid so," he admitted.

"How do you know?" demanded the sheriff.

"By the merest chance," Tuck explained, and went on to tell how the guard had rushed from the castle, terrified of the raving prisoner, his sores and the stench.

"The prisoner can't have the plague!" cried the sheriff. "He has seen no one – for weeks!"

"A good point, sir" Tuck agreed, "but plague is a mysterious thing It pops up – from nowhere – at odd times. Some say rats carry the disease. Would there be a few rats down there, sir?" The sheriff was thinking. This news must not leak out; nor the identity of the prisoner. If only Sir Richard would die, and quickly. If only . . .

Friar Tuck watched the sheriff's face and read the working of his devious mind.

"Where's my guard now?" asked the sheriff.

Tuck hesitated. "My lord sheriff, I'm afraid I usurped your authority and had him shut up for the time being, in the care of a brother friar. At least, he'll not be causing panic . . . When your prisoner dies, he may be dead now, well, that could be the end of it . . . I hope I did the right thing, sir?"

The sheriff actually smiled his approval. "You acted wisely, my good friar, very wisely. Have you any other suggestions to help us out of this mess?"

Protesting modestly, Friar Tuck mentioned a few more ideas; ones that Robin had thought up; ideas that would help to get Sir Richard out of Nottingham Castle.

Robin becomes a guard

Back in The Glen, Robin and Little John waited to hear the friar's horse clopping towards the widow's cottage. They were alert and ready when the guard brought it to the barn. Turning to go, the man found his way barred by a tall monk and an old woman.

"Don't be afraid," said Little John. "Friar Tuck has asked me to help you. Give the woman her key."

The guard was too amazed to question anything; he just did as he was told. Inside, Robin brought mead while John sat talking.

"Please tell me your name?" he asked.

"Gunter. I'm a guard at the castle. Help me, Father! I don't want to die!"

"You won't die, Gunter, if you do as I suggest. Your clothes, now, they're contaminated. Let's burn them, shall we? Mother!" he called to Robin. "Bring some old clothes, please!"

The clothes Robin had been wearing were thrown into the room and the guard put them on. John took Gunter's to the barn where Robin dressed himself as the guard.

"Gunter," said John as he came back, "you stay here. Keep the doors locked. If the sheriff overlooks your lapse of duty, I'll bring a fresh uniform. If he wants you taken in charge – well, I'll lose my prisoner. How's that?" He clapped Gunter on the shoulder, laughing as he went.

Robin was waiting in the cart and they made for the castle – just a guard on an errand for the sheriff, and a priest having a ride into town.

The butcher's cart

Out on the castle ramparts, the sheriff and Friar Tuck were talking and enjoying the fresh air. Tuck had manoeuvred this to give him a view of the road. He asked if he might be allowed to visit the prisoner. The sheriff didn't want this; Tuck might recognize Sir Richard. "If that deserting guard were here," he declared, "I'd send him down to deal with things. More contact wouldn't matter – for him."

"Of course," agreed the friar, "you are perfectly right! I'll bring him back. Give me his orders, my lord, there's no sense in your taking risks."

The sheriff thought this an excellent idea. The guard could cover the body and get it away through the grid in the outside wall.

"He knows the grid – he has the keys. Don't you go down, my good friar," went on the sheriff. "Meet him in the lane and lead him to a suitable place. Just get rid of that body. Make him take the passage behind the stables. I don't want him taking a short-cut through the kitchens."

"Put your mind at rest, sir, he shall obey every detail," said the friar.

In the very nick of time, the cart came bumping towards the castle.

"Heaven be praised!" cried Tuck earnestly. "See that? Your guard has come to his senses. He's returning to serve you! Sheriff, you must feel proud to command such loyalty. I'll give your orders at once. My brother friar and I will conduct the last rites and give him Christian Committal – not to the earth, sir, but to fire. I'm sorry, my lord, it is the only safe way."

The sheriff nodded. He could hardly believe his good fortune. "God bless us all," he murmured.

"Amen," added Friar Tuck in all sincerity and sped down to the courtyard.

Little John drove the cart to the grid. Robin walked to the passage behind the stables. Tuck looked up; the sheriff was watching. Tuck moved away. Then, when the sheriff turned, he slipped through the kitchen to join Robin down below.

The sheriff strolled along the ramparts to find a good viewing place. He just had to see Sir Richard's last journey from Nottingham Castle.

Difficulties

Down in the dungeon, the prisoner waited patiently. After the guard had rushed off, leaving the door open, a slight draught had fanned his face. It felt wonderful.

He was too weak to reach the stairs; besides, what good was that? Robin had promised — that promise would be kept.

When Sir Richard heard footsteps his heart began to thump. He couldn't breathe; spasms shook him. He trembled and gasped. He really was dying.

"Oh, God," he cried, "let me live to see the forest — to breathe pure air — just once!"

Robin was suddenly at his side.

"You will, Sir Richard," he whispered. "But hush now, you are supposed to be dead. Friar Tuck and I are putting you in this sack and carrying you out to a cart. You will lie hidden by logs of wood until we reach the forest. Keep still, I beg you. It will seem a long time, I'm afraid; we have to act out a mock funeral. Not a word now. We're ready."

Trying to hold their breath against the stench, they carried the pallet bearing Sir Richard's body out of the door. Robin took the keys from the lock and they turned past the stairs. Dark tunnels spread right and left. Dear God, which one? Far ahead shone a tiny gleam — it was the grid and daylight!

The slimy, uneven ground rose in a slope to reach the level of the outside world. A step — and stop . . . steady, and step again. They must keep on their feet . . . At last! They put the pallet down and Robin tried the keys. The third one turned — but the grid wouldn't move. Set half-way up, it needed a weight to swing the upper part down, and the lower half out into the lane.

"Get on my back," Robin said to Tuck. "When you have a good grip, I'll collapse. Your weight should move it." It was exhausting work. A face appeared at the grid.

"I'll pull up while you pull down" It was Little John! With his help the grid swung open.

The pallet was lifted up and out. Then Robin was out. Turning to help Tuck, they saw that he'd never squeeze through.

They were silent. Suddenly Tuck started to chuckle.

"What is there to laugh about?" cried Robin.

"We've been saved from a big mistake. I was told not to come down here. The sheriff's bound to be watching. I'll go back and come by the road." And Tuck slithered into darkness.

From the castle heights, the sheriff saw the pallet placed in the cart. Yes, there was the still form — a body in a sack.

The guard and the priest covered
it with what looked like logs.
   As the extraordinary procession
moved away it was joined by a
well pleased, but rather
breathless Friar Tuck.

The funeral pyre

The sheriff was so delighted, he thought he'd see things to the very end. Shouting for his horse, he then followed the funeral to the forest.

Little John turned to grin at Robin and Tuck as they walked behind.

"No rejoicing yet," warned Robin. "The sheriff may be having us watched. I'm his runaway guard, remember?"

"You're right, master," John apologized. "We are being followed now – by the mighty one himself."

"So," said Robin, "he has come to check on you, Tuck, and to kill his guard. We need the last bit of our plan after all. Did you and Greenwood make the escape hole at the cave, Little John?"

"Yes, master."

"And are my clothes with Mistress Greenwood?" Robin asked.

"Everything is ready, master," he answered.

"I don't like it, Robin," put in Tuck. "You could suffocate, or fall into the fire. We shan't even know what's happening."

"Just pray hard," replied Robin.

A short distance from the hovel, John backed the cart and dragged open the door. Then, gathering brushwood and sticks, he and Robin built a fire in the middle. Friar Tuck stood by the cart. Somehow, Sir Richard had to be moved off the pallet and the deer carcase put in his place. After building the fire the two men came one on each side of the cart, while Tuck climbed up and knelt facing the body. Raising his arms, the friar chanted his prayers. His wide sleeves and huge body provided a shield behind which John and Robin were able to make the change.

The service was over and the pallet and carcase were in position – soon to be hidden by billowing smoke and fierce flames. As Robin turned from the cave, he glanced at the sheriff; then, as if terrified, he threw up his arms and with a scream leapt into the burning hovel. John dived in after him, but was driven back, choking and spluttering.

The friar and John knelt down. They weren't mocking their faith, but praying sincerely for Robin's safety. Then, going to the hovel, they closed the sagging door.

"Drive to the valley, John. I'll detain the sheriff," said Tuck. He lifted his hand, acknowledging the sheriff and walked towards him.

The sheriff, however, was satisfied; he had no wish for further conversation. He turned his horse and rode back to Nottingham Castle.

Robin in danger

In the cave, Robin dropped on all fours and crawled to the back. Through the roof, there was the tunnel-shaped hole with a ledge to grip round the base of its wall.

He reached up – in vain – he wasn't tall enough!

"Oh, Little John!" he cried out, "we're not all giants like you!"

Near the ground, John had made a niche for his foot, but he needed something to grip with his hand. He tried again, but it was no good.

Between eddies of smoke, the light showed tiny roots trailing from the newly dug soil. A root? He immediately started feeling, high on the wall, tracing a bulge, a thick line. Off came the guard's belt as Robin scraped frantically with the buckle.

The heat scorched him and the smoke was blinding; but he'd found what he wanted. With more earth picked away, he had a loop – a strong handle. He tested it; it would hold.

With his foot in the niche, he swung up. He reached and held the ledge with one hand, brought his foot from the niche to push on the root, and he was up into the tunnel. Then, clutching some plant stems, he dragged himself onto the cool green surface.

He gulped great mouthfuls of air as he lay gazing at the trees. How many times he'd depended on them. Now, even a humble root had saved his life.

He crept away, to change his clothes at the Greenwoods' cave. With the guard's uniform pushed down into the fire, Robin made for home. He was worn·out, but when he saw Sir Richard his spirits lifted.

The widow had bathed and clothed Sir Richard in fresh linen. He lay under a shelter of young saplings on a bed of sweet-smelling bracken – and he slept. Every risk, every hardship they had suffered was as nothing in view of this. The plan had worked – Sir Richard was alive and with friends.

The end of the guard

Two days later, Friar Tuck took the widow home. The men waved goodbye and Robin promised that she should come again to see her sons. They found the cottage unlocked and the guard gone. He had left the borrowed garments and taken a few things belonging to her eldest son. A neighbour came along with a message.

"Your friend said he felt well, and he thanked you both. You'll find your horse at The Anvil, south of the forest. And 'God bless you,' he said. I think that was all, Father."

Tuck gave her a beaming smile. "I'm sure you've remembered every word. Thank you."

So, good luck to Gunter! He had taken his chance. No man could expect understanding from the sheriff of Nottingham – let alone a guard who left his post. The widow was glad to be back, and happy now, about her sons.

Friar Tuck collected his horse the next day and rode to the castle. With the sheriff away on his judicial circuit, he'd have an opportunity to speak to Maid Marion. He couldn't tell her the true story about her father, but he did say that when the king returned, Sir Richard would come home too.

They spoke of the tournament. "Will it be safe for Robin Hood to come?" Marion asked. "My guardian boasts of capturing him.

Some trap is being prepared, now. Seamstresses are making habits, for monks! I don't know any more, but will you warn Robin?"

"I will, my lady, and thank you." Tuck came away in deep thought. What was his lordship up to? Would it happen soon, or at the tournament, in a month's time? Would Sir Richard be well by then? Would he be able to face the sheriff, and bring him to his knees? Robin and Tuck talked late into the night, trying to answer all the questions.

Sir Richard sets a target

Sir Richard was making good progress. He was now able to walk to the butts where Robin and his men were training for the tournament.

One day he offered to set them a target, and asked for a willow wand to be put up.

"The first man to split the wand three times may claim a prize from me!" he declared.

That triggered them off, laughing and fooling about.

"The prize is mine!" boasted Little John. "Save your strength and give in gracefully!"

"Gracefully?" questioned Scarlet. He took Will Stutely by the hand and with mincing steps they danced down the greensward.

"Get out of the way, you two willows!" roared Tuck. "I'll make four of you!" He raised his bow and they dived for safety.

Then they were quiet and got down to business. Friar Tuck split the wand with his third arrow; Little John with his second; and the others fell short. Then it was Robin's turn. His first split the foot of the willow; his second pierced the middle, and the third lodged between that and the top. The men were delighted. Robin was their hero – he must succeed – always.

The contest was over. Sir Richard returned to his shelter to rest; the men to their other duties.

As for Robin, he wandered away, to think. There was a prize he wanted from Sir Richard – a valuable one. He wanted to marry Maid Marion. But how could an outlaw dare to make such a request?

A strange visitor

Robin was completely absorbed. He didn't even see the strangers until they were quite close. Three monks! He remembered Marion's warning. Were these the sheriff's men out to capture him? They rode proud stallions, and wore fine cloth; and they had a distinct air of authority – strange monks indeed!

If only I could pull off their cowls, he thought, and see who they really are.

He strode forward, leisurely.

"You travel slowly. Are you lost?" he asked politely. "Not lost," answered the tallest monk, who rode in the middle, "but rather bewildered. We were told to expect cutthroats, brawling outlaws; we find the forest quiet and peaceful. Have you ever met any robbers, friend?"

"I know the outlaws well, Father, but I'd hardly call them cutthroats and robbers."

"No? How would you describe them? Perhaps your are one yourself?" said the monk sharply.

"Yes I am," replied Robin, "and fortunate to be with such brave, loyal men."

The monk laughed scornfully. "You choose the wrong words, surely? They are outside the law; they steal King Richard's deer, and rob travellers of their last penny!"

Robin smiled. "May I correct you on two points, kind sirs," he began. "First, no traveller is left without money to complete his journey. Second, these men have been driven outside the law by unscrupulous barons and officials. As for the deer, would King Richard deny his archers food? Right here, he has a small army ready and skilled to fight for him. He could never find better bowmen!"

The monk was impressed. "You interest me, young sir," he declared. "Would it be possible to meet these men and their leader?"

Robin laughed. "Nothing more possible! Allow me." He lifted his horn and blew just once. In seconds, there stood Little John, Will Scarlet and Will Stutely.

"Would you permit these men to blindfold you?" Robin asked. "No outsider is allowed to see the position of our camp."

The tall monk smiled to himself. "This outlaw, this Robin Hood," he asked, "is it true he is a man of breeding?"

Robin looked straight into the eyes above the cowl.
"That is for you to decide, Father. I am Robin Hood. Will you join us at supper? But, let me warn you, you will pay for the meal and remember, you too, will be stealing the king's deer."
The monk threw back his head and laughed. He liked this outlaw.

Round the camp fire, wine was served.

"A toast, gentlemen!" cried Robin. "To our king! Richard the Lion Heart! Let no man drink who would not defend, or fight with him. May he soon be back in his own country. God bless King Richard!"

Everyone drained his goblet; it was a solemn moment.

"Now," said Robin in a more jovial voice, "may we see who our guests are? Please remove your cowls and hoods, kind sirs."

As they slowly did so there was a gasp from the assembled outlaws. Sir Richard was the first to come forward to kneel before the tallest monk. Robin knelt too.

Every man followed suit and the cry went round: "God bless King Richard!"

The king, for he it was, was touched by their sincerity.

"Come!" he tossed his head, inviting them to stand. "We have royal venison to eat, and I'm hungry!" He grinned at Robin then turned to Sir Richard. "You have been ill, my friend?" he asked. "I looked for you in France."

"It's a long story, sire," put in Robin. "May we tell you later?"

Supper began with the outlaws entertaining their king! And King Richard enjoying the company of outlaws – it was fantastic! Before darkness fell, the outlaws were asked to show their skills in archery. The splitting of the willow fascinated the king.

"I need you to train my bowmen," he said. "But not as an outlaw. Kneel down, Robin, and hand me your sword."

There and then, Robin was knighted; his freedom and his property were restored.

"Arise, Sir Robin of Locksley!" declared the king. "And all you good-for-nothings," and they laughed, "you are now the King's Own Foresters. You, Master Little John shall keep them in order. See to it!"

The boisterous party simmered down. King Richard retired to his bed of bracken; night and the forest enveloped them all. Robin went, as usual, to see that Sir Richard was all right. "What a day, Robin! Shall we ever enjoy another like it?"

"I hope so," said Robin. "I'll be back every year on this date. I shall never forget my men of Sherwood."

"By the way," Sir Richard reminded him, "you have a prize to claim. Have you had time to think about it?"

"I have thought about it for a long time, Sir Richard," said Robin, seriously. "Now that I am no longer an outlaw, may I ask for your daughter's hand in marriage?" Sir Richard looked at Robin. He loved him as a son; there could be no better suitor for Maid Marion. He grasped his hand.

"What a day!" he repeated. "This just crowns it all!"

The Royal Procession

Before King Richard left for Nottingham Castle, next morning, he knew the whole story of Sir Richard's imprisonment. For the present it would be kept secret, and the fact that he had met Robin and pardoned the outlaws. Mounted and ready, the king turned to Friar Tuck.

"If you ever need a new habit," he said, "try the tall building in town. Makers to the king — no less!"

The men were still laughing as he rode out of sight.

Nottingham was bursting at the seams. Visitors had come for the tournament, for the yearly Goose Fair, and for a chance to see the king. Cattle, horses, pigs and geese had been driven from miles around. Bands of minstrels entertained; players performed miracle plays; dancing bears and freaks earned a few pence. The coming week would be a glorious hotch-potch of splendour, poverty and excitement.

When the opening day arrived, soldiers rode the streets making a gangway for the royal procession. This stretched from the castle to the lists, where the jousting, wrestling and archery would take place. The royal stand, tiers of seats and various tents had been erected.

Outriders and heralds led the colourful procession in gorgeous uniforms, their horses draped in silks and gold. Flags and banners waved; plumes tossed and harnesses flashed and jingled. King Richard, splendid on his black stallion, turned and smiled at the crowd, acknowledging the cheers.

The sheriff and his retinue came next, followed by Lady Marion and her ladies, with the wives of the competitors. Barons, knights and their squires headed a long line of riders. Guy of Gisbourne looked round. He was interested in a group of men in Lincoln green . . . And who was the handsome fellow in front? The question kept nagging him. As the procession entered the enclosure the stranger looked straight at Gisbourne. It was Robin Hood.

How dare he flaunt himself here in his finery? But what a chance! He'd been waiting a long time for this.

This is my day, thought the baron. I will take my revenge.

Robin rode to the royal stand, faced the king and bowed; then his mount, a beautiful grey, pawed the ground and lowered its head. Richard was delighted, and people clapped. As Robin backed away, he flashed a smile to Maid Marion. She too, was puzzled until she saw Friar Tuck and the men in green.

Marion was deeply afraid for Robin. He might be arrested and disgraced in front of the king!

Robin's smile had been noticed. "One of your admirers, Lady Marion?" King Richard teased her. Hardly knowing what she was doing, she spoke up for Robin. "Your majesty, if anyone speaks ill of him, it will be false. He is a good man and loyal to you!"

"My dear Lady Marion," the king answered, "I'll form my own opinion. But I'm sure he'd be happy to hear yours."

A great fanfare blared out. The jousting was about to begin.

The Tournament

Two contesting knights waited at opposite ends of the lists. Armour and crested shields were gleaming; proud horses, wearing leather caparisons, tossed their heads impatiently; a massive lance was passed to each rider by his own squire.

The trumpet blared again; the knights thundered down the course. They swerved not an inch and collided with an ear-splitting crash! Then came thrust and counter-thrust at helmet and shield. A knight swayed but remained seated. On to the end, reining in and turning. Then, with a fresh lance, they galloped off on their second course. Jeers and cheers rewarded each blow.

On the fourth run, the same knight reeled and dropped from his saddle. A Norman down!... The Saxons yelled with delight. Jousting went on for hours and would continue to do so throughout the week.

In the wrestling matches, Friar Tuck and Little John were a great attraction. What a pair, and how they played to the crowd! Like sacks of wheat they dumped each other to the ground. Thump! And thump! They never tired. The onlookers were more exhausted — with laughing! At last, the king held up his hand; the contest was over. It was a tie, he declared.

After several other fights and displays the archery event was announced. This was the highlight of the day and each heat was watched closely. When the finalists lined up, there were six of them; two strangers, Guy of Gisbourne, Little John, Friar Tuck and Robin Hood. There was nothing to choose between them; all six scored bullseyes.

Once more the king raised his hand. He ordered the willow-wand targets to be set up. Each competitor would have three shots and aim at his own particular wand.

A hush fell as the first stranger took aim. All three arrows fell short. The second man split the wand once. Guy of Gisbourne put two on target, and Little John equalled him. Then a shout went up for the fat friar; he had captured the affection of them all.

It seemed he took aim almost carelessly but all three arrows split the willow. The cheers were deafening; men danced and waved like children.

Thank goodness for Tuck, Robin thought. One of us at least has beaten Gisbourne. Then Robin took aim: the base . . . The middle . . . The top — all split cleanly. The crowd went wild. What now? Surely, no further tests: But some wags wanted more.

"Here, masters," cried one, "put your arrows through this!" And he threw his cap in the air.

Robin and Tuck grinned at each other and let fly. Both pierced the cloth; the cap dropped to the ground. Roars of appreciation ended the contest. It couldn't have been better.

Later, Robin sat talking to Maid Marion in the royal stand. "Are you enjoying the fun?" he asked.

"Very much," she answered. "But how is it, Robin Hood, that you are here in the lion's mouth,

and just asking to be arrested?"

Robin laughed. "I'll explain — one day. Just now, the sheriff is puzzled. He doesn't know how I rate with the king; he won't do anything drastic."

Maid Marion congratulated him on the archery and asked him to bring Friar Tuck to see her. "I'm fond of him," she said. "He's been a good friend."

On his way to find the friar, Robin came suddenly face-to-face with Gisbourne. They met behind the canvas which backed all the tiers of seats. There was no one about. Gisbourne drew his sword.

"I have a score to settle," he hissed.

"Maybe," Robin replied, "but I have no sword."

"Too bad," sneered the baron. "Take mine, as you did my whip." He was after Robin ready to kill.

Robin could rely only on his speed. He backed, putting himself, it seemed, at a disadvantage. Now he was almost up against the canvas. He dodged — right, left and left again. Now his enemy was off balance. Diving down, he tackled Gisbourne at knee-level, and tossed him into the canvas. The sword stuck in the wooden struts . . . Gisbourne nearly exploded with rage.

Robin stood over him — laughing. Then he blew one long note on his horn and before Gisbourne was on his feet, there stood Little John, Will Scarlet and Will Stutely with Friar Tuck behind, being pulled along by two of his giant dogs.

"What shall we do with him, master?" asked Stutely.

"Chase him off!" cried Robin.

Tuck had Gisbourne's sword and went after him playfully. In his confusion, Gisbourne took the wrong turn at the end of the canvas wall; he suddenly found himself in the lists in full view of the spectators. These must have thought the chase was a bit of friendly fooling. To see the enormous friar prodding a Norman noble in the rear, and trying to hold back a pair of ferocious hounds ready to eat him, was quite the funniest thing ever. The crowd rocked! It was Tuck's day all right. Everybody loved him. The two figures raced round and out of the field, while waves of laughter brought the day's sport to an unforgettable, and hilarious end.

The fall of the Sheriff

Things weren't going right for the sheriff at all. His plan, put to the king at Newark, recently, had misfired. The three monks had, apparently, come through the forest unmolested. Then, during the tournament, the king and Robin Hood had become friends. How could he risk upsetting the king by arresting the outlaw?

And Gisbourne? He was no use! Not a sign of him since he'd made such an exhibition of himself. The tournament banquet was due to begin that very night, and nothing had been achieved. But it will be, thought the sheriff, I'll bring Robin Hood down in front of the whole assembly!

He gave instructions that, whatever the outlaw called himself, he must be announced as "Robin Hood." That would create a stir!

Guests were arriving; the great hall was a mass of colour and elegance. Any minute now . . . Two figures were at the door, and a voice proclaimed: "Knights attending the King! Sir Richard of Lea! Sir Robin of Locksley!"

What fool's trick was this? Sir Richard had no son! And why had his final orders been disregarded?

He could do nothing at that moment, for here was the king. "Our gracious majesty, King Richard the Lion-Heart! God save the king!"

The ladies curtsied; the men bowed; the sheriff stole a glance at the older knight. Terror clutched at his heart . . . The lights swam . . . It was the ghost of Sir Richard! Nothing else was visible. Just a ball of light floating towards him. . . . The ghost of his old friend.

The sheriff backed away. "No!" he screamed. "No! No!" He tried to run, but he couldn't move. The ghost and shadows closed in . . . Down he sank, gibbering and crying for mercy.

From high above him came a loud voice: "Let him suffer as he made my friend, Sir Richard, suffer. To the dungeons with him — now!" Hands grabbed him; marched him; hurled him. Bolts grated; locks were turned.

He was alone in the unspeakable horrors of darkness and filth. "He can cool his heels for awhile," the king decided. "But the banquet and our friends are here — we shall enjoy both."

Before the evening was over plans were made for Robin's future; his duties in the king's army, and his marriage with Maid Marion.

Spring in Sherwood Forest

Spring came round once more and the forest was dressed in green. It was Robin's wedding day. There in the clearing, he and Maid Marion stood in front of Friar Tuck. Sir Richard, the Merry Men, Alan-a-Dale and hundreds of villagers — even Tuck's famous dogs, all were there to wish them well. With the sheriff banished for life, and Gisbourne not seen for months, there was nothing to spoil their day.

In the silence of the great forest, Friar Tuck began the marriage service.

Suddenly, Saxon leapt into the air, caught something and laid it at Marion's feet.

It was an arrow . . .

Robin gazed at the murderous weapon. Then the friar held the feathered tip to Saxon's nose, gave a command and the dog was off.

"He will find him," said Tuck.

"So will I!" cried Robin as he pushed his way past the groups of friends.

Saxon had picked up the scent and was racing ahead. Diving

under low branches, and tearing himself free of the brambles, Robin was hard pressed to keep up. Will Scarlet and Little John followed; they might be needed. Just as Robin thought he had lost the dog, there it was — head lowered, teeth bared, snarling at the fugitive cut off by dense undergrowth.

Gisbourne!

"Move one finger and he'll tear your throat out!" Robin warned. Robin drew closer. How he wished he'd learned Tuck's way of talking to his dogs. He wanted Gisbourne for himself. Would Saxon obey him? If he didn't, things could be disastrous.

Will Scarlet's voice came from behind him.

"When you're ready, master, I'll call him off."

Robin drew his sword. "Right, Will. I'm ready!"

"Now, Saxon, here!" Will spoke quietly, as Tuck always did. The dog went down, still watching Gisbourne, but allowing Will to slip his belt through its collar.

"Draw!" demanded Robin. Gisbourne drew his sword. Robin had begun his fiercest ever fight. Will led Saxon out of range; the space must be clear — every inch of it. The men slashed and parried, backed and lunged, side-stepped and feinted. Every trick in the book came into the struggle; a struggle that could only end in death — possibly for both of them.

Gisbourne was the bigger, heavier and slower man. Robin danced round him, but both were wounded; the pace was beginning to tell. Suddenly, Robin tripped; he was on his back, his sword out of reach.

"God help him!" prayed Will and John together.

Gisbourne paused triumphantly, delaying just a second too long.

With all his strength, Robin slammed his horn straight into Gisbourne's face. Then, he was up and ready once more.

Blood splashed and dust rose as they blundered and staggered. How long could it go on? Will and John hardly breathed. Must they stand by and see Robin killed? It was his fight . . . so they clenched their teeth — and waited.

Gradually the fight grew more skilful. And Robin was now winning. New energy surged through him; a mighty sweep sent Gisbourne's sword flying into the bushes. Robin heaved mightily downwards and the deed was done. Gisbourne would not torture or persecute anyone again.

A great cheer went up as Robin and Saxon returned. The day had started as one of rejoicing; now, with both Robin and Marion safe, it was even happier.

Robin's last arrow

Robin served King Richard faithfully; he won renown in battle and was made Earl of Huntingdon for his valour.

When Richard was killed in France, Robin's interest turned from battlefields to the fields of home. He had no wish to serve King John so he went back to his lands, and settled down as lord of the manor.

His old friends were never forgotten. Friar Tuck was still his adviser and companion. He often stayed at Robin and Marion's home, delighting their children with tales of Sherwood days.

Little John and Will Scarlet kept an inn, out Ollerton way, and when possible rode through the forest. When Robin felt the pull of Sherwood he would go alone, follow the glades, and linger at the special landmarks.

On one, such a day, Robin left his horse at The Anvil and walked to the deserted camp. He was not well — he was suffering from a touch of fever he had contracted during the wars. At the great oak, he was glad to sink down onto the ground. He longed for his friends — if only he could summon them! Instinctively he raised his horn and gave three blasts.

Little John was riding on the edge of the forest. He could hardly believe his ears — that famous horn blaring once more! He wondered if he were going mad.

Mad or not, he had to answer the call. He galloped to the tree and found Robin lying there.

"Oh, master!" he cried. "What can I do for you?"

"Little John, it's good to see you. Get me to Kirklees. The Prioress of the nunnery is a relative of mine. She is skilled in medicine and will bleed me. Hurry, John."

The Prioress admitted Robin and allowed Little John to carry tower. Then he was ordered to leave. John was determined to stay as near as possible, so he settled outside, at the foot of the tower.

The Prioress, an ambitious nun, saw a chance to curry favour with King John. What if she got rid of this one-time outlaw, still a threat to and an enemy of the king? She bled Robin and left him locked in his room. With a cut artery it doesn't take long to bleed to death.

Robin, rousing a little from his weakness, realized what she had done. He crawled to the slit in the wall and blew a faint note on his horn. Little John was up and forcing his way past the nuns. With all his strength he burst open the door to find his master dying.

"Bring my bow, John," he whispered. "Help me up . . . Where this arrow falls . . . there let me lie . . . Bury me with my bow by my side . . ."
Robin shot his arrow and sank back into Little John's arms. Bowed down with grief John carried out his master's wishes.

The grave was green each spring; dappled in the summer sun; russet and gold in autumn; white with winter's snow.

★ ★ ★

Robin Hood may have died hundreds of years ago, but in the hearts of those who love to hear his story — his spirit will never die.